Lucky Break

Peter Millett Toby Quarmby

Lucky Break

Text: Peter Millet
Illustrations: Toby Quarmby
Editor: Rebecca Crisp
Design: James Lowe
Series design: James Lowe
Production controller: Lisa Porter
Reprint: Siew Han Ong

Fast Forward Independent Texts
Level 18

ISBN 978 0 17 017974 4
ISBN 978 0 17 017898 3 (set)

Cengage Learning Australia
Level 7, 80 Dorcas Street
South Melbourne, Victoria Australia 3205
Phone: 1300 790 853

Cengage Learning New Zealand
Unit 4B Rosedale Office Park
331 Rosedale Road, Albany, North Shore NZ 0632
Phone: 0508 635 766

For learning solutions, visit **cengage.com.au**

Printed in Australia by Ligare Pty Ltd
3 4 5 23 22 21

Lucky Break

Peter Millett Toby Quarmby

Contents

Surf's Up

Matt and Corban sat on their surfboards, waiting for the next wave to come in.

"Hey Matt, how much more money do you need to enter the *Big Break* surfing competition?" asked Corban.

"A lot more.
How about you, Corban?" Matt said.

"Same – I'll have to mow lawns
day and night
to pay for a ticket," Corban complained.

Just then a big wave rolled in.
"Mine!" Matt cried.

Matt raced down the face of the wave,
but the wave broke too early
and he was wiped out.
He jumped back to his feet.

"Ow!" he yelled,
as he put his foot down.

"What is it?" Corban cried.

"I stood on a rock!
Man, that really hurt," Matt said.
He jumped back on his board.
"Stay away from that part of the beach!"

Treasure Found

Later when the tide had gone out, Matt and Corban walked back up the beach.

"Hey, there's that rock I stood on," Matt said angrily.

Corban took a closer look. "That's not a rock – it's a box."

"Man, it looks really old. It must have been in the sea forever," said Matt.

"What do you think is inside it?" Corban asked.

"Maybe gold?" Matt hoped.

Corban's eyes lit up.

"Cool!

I'll never have to mow

another lawn again!" he yelled.

The boys tried opening the box,

but they couldn't.

"It's locked," said Matt.
"Let's take it home.
Maybe we can break it open
with one of my dad's tools."

Matt and Corban each took
an end of the box
and lifted it up onto Matt's surfboard.

CHAPTER 3

Finders, Keepers

When they arrived home,
Matt's dad did a double-take.

"What on Earth is that?" Dad asked.

"We found a treasure box
on the beach," Matt said.

"A treasure box?" Dad asked.

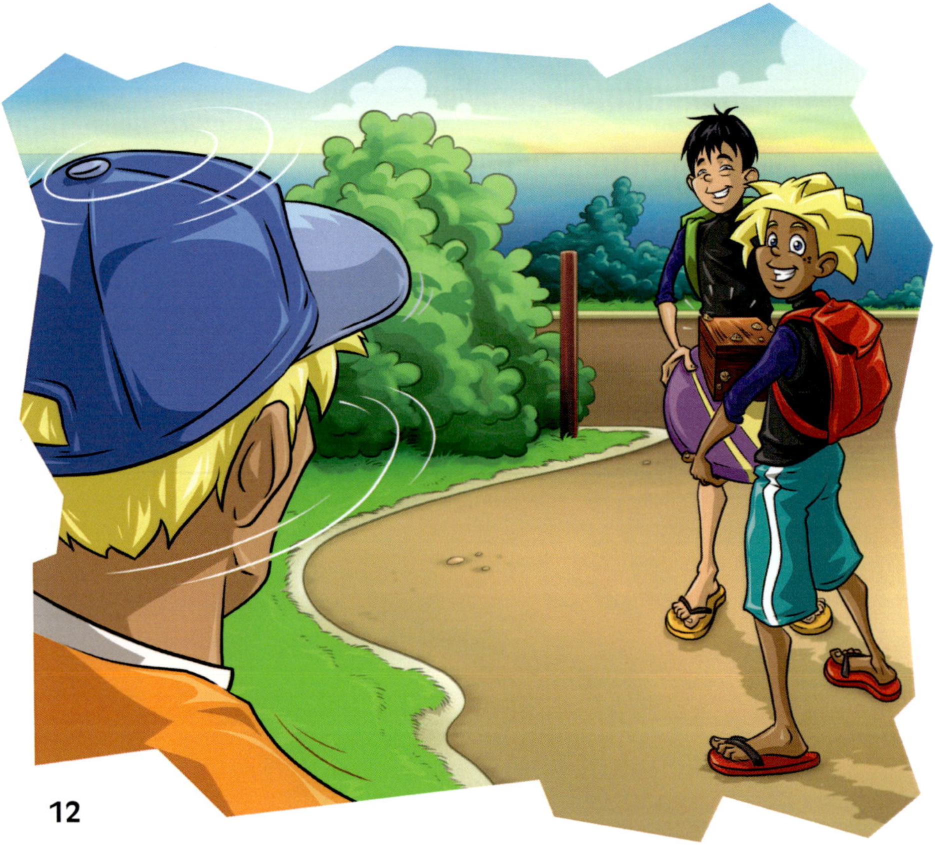

"What made you think
it was yours to take home?" Dad said.

Matt looked at Corban.
"Why not?
Remember that man on TV last year?
He got to keep all those coins
he found on that old ship," Matt said.

"Yes," Dad said.
"But he went to a lot of trouble to get those coins.
He spent six weeks looking in shark-filled waters before he found them.
What did you do to find the box?"

"I stood on it," Matt muttered.

"Anyway we're going to sell
what's in the box,
and use the money to enter
the *Big Break* surfing competition,"
Corban said.

Matt's dad scratched his head.
"But what if there's something important in the box?
Something that other people might like to see?
Maybe you should think about giving it to the Sea Research Centre," he said.

What to Do?

That night Matt and Corban couldn't sleep for thinking about the box.

Was it right to keep it?
Or should they give the box
to the Sea Research Centre instead?

The following morning Corban and Matt made up their minds.

"Dad, maybe you're right.
The box doesn't belong to us.
How about you take us down
to the Sea Research Centre?" Matt said.

"Sure thing," Dad said, smiling.

The captain at the Sea Research Centre
was over the moon
when Matt and Corban gave him
the box.

"Fantastic, boys!
Thank you!" the captain cried.

"Do you think there's gold inside?"
Corban asked.

The captain smiled.
"If there is,
you'll be the first to know," he said.

A few days later,
an email arrived
from the Sea Research Centre.

The boys' faces dropped
when they saw the photo attached.

"Oh man, there was only an old telescope inside the box," Matt said.

Dad stared at the screen.
"But look, it says here
that it's the only one like it
in the whole world.
How amazing is that?
Now everyone will get to see
what you found."

Real Treasure

Just then there was a knock at the door.

A man handed over a gold box.

"What's this?" Corban asked.

Matt read the attached note.
"It's from the Sea Research Centre,"
he told Corban.

"Open it! Open it!" Corban cried.
Matt opened the box.

Inside were two tickets
to the *Big Break* surfing competition.

"Awesome!" Matt cried.
He gave his friend a high-five.

"See, we did find treasure after all!"
Corban laughed.